LAURENCE ANHOLT is one of the most prestigious authors
writing for children today. His previous books for Frances Lincoln
include the **Anholt's Artists** series featuring
Van Gogh, Degas, Picasso, Leonardo da Vinci and Monet.
Together with his wife Catherine, he wrote and illustrated
the Nestlé Smarties Gold Award-winning book **Chimp and Zee**,
which was followed by **Chimp and Zee and the Big Storm**
and **Happy Birthday Chimp and Zee.**
Laurence lives with his family in Dorset, England.

JIM COPLESTONE studied Graphic Illustration
at Exeter College of Art and completed an MA in Theatre Design.
He has worked as a primary school teacher, arts workshop leader
and home tutor, and his rapport with children
is apparent in his lively pictures.
Jim's first book for Frances Lincoln was **Noah's Bed**,
written by his wife Lis. Jim lives with his family in Dorset, England.

For Pop Read, who sat me on his lap when I was three
and showed me how to draw a sparrow – J.C.

Seven for a Secret copyright © Frances Lincoln Limited 2006
Text copyright © Laurence Anholt 2006
Illustrations copyright © Jim Coplestone 2006

The right of Laurence Anholt to be identified as the Author of this work
has been asserted by him in accordance with the Copyright, Designs and Patents Act, 1988.

First published in Great Britain and the USA in 2006 by
Frances Lincoln Children's Books, 4 Torriano Mews,
Torriano Avenue, London NW5 2RZ
www.franceslincoln.com

Distributed in the USA by Publishers Group West

First paperback edition published in Great Britain and the USA in 2007

A version of this story was first published under the title **The Magpie Song**
in 1995 by Egmont Children's Books.

British Library Cataloguing in Publication Data available on request

ISBN 10: 1-84507-590-0
ISBN 13: 978-1-84507-590-3

Illustrated with watercolour and crayon

Printed in Singapore

1 3 5 7 9 8 6 4 2

Visit the Anholts' magical bookshop **Chimp and Zee, Bookshop by the Sea**,
51 Broad Street, Lyme Regis, DT7 3SQ or shop online at www.anholt.co.uk

Seven
for a
Secret

Laurence Anholt
Illustrated by Jim Coplestone

F

FRANCES LINCOLN
CHILDREN'S BOOKS

Dear Grampa,

It's noisy in the city and I can't sleep.
I hear police cars, a dog barking and the TV next door.
I see a million orange lights below.
I thought about you far away in the countryside.
Will you visit us one day?
Will you write to me?

Good night,

Ruby

Dear Ruby,

Thank you for your letter. It is so cold today that I read it by the fire.

There's a lot of squawking going on outside. A big family of magpies lives in the hollow tree by my window. I'll tell you a secret — I can peep right inside their nest.

Do you know the Magpie Song? I've written it down just for you.

This is the song I sang to your daddy when he was a little boy.

I think about you every day, high in our apartment. I'd like to visit one day.

Send my love to everyone.

Grampa

THE MAGPIE SONG
(for my Ruby in the city)

1 for Sorrow,
2 for Joy,
3 for a Girl,
4 for a Boy,
5 for Silver,
6 for Gold,
7 for a Secret
never to be told.

Dear Grampa,

It's been cold here too. Mum and I got freezing waiting for the bus.

The lift isn't working and we had to carry the shopping up all 574 steps.

When we got in, Dad had already gone to work.

Did it snow where you are?
Are there wild animals in the woods?

Love from

Ruby

My dearest Ruby,

The woods are magical when it snows –
as white as the pages of a book. It tells you
the whole story of the night before if you know
how to read it. The words are animal footprints.

These marks are from a fox out hunting:

and these are where some deer
have crossed the lawn:

and these are the marks of those naughty old
magpies taking all the food from my bird table:

There were three magpies this morning –
3 for a girl. That's why I thought of you.

With fondest love,

Grampa.

Dear Grampa,

Dad says there are foxes in the city too. They live under the railway bridge. He says you see all kinds of secret things when you work nights.

Some people sleep down there because they don't have anywhere else to go.

I asked Dad about the Magpie Song but he said he didn't remember. He says he will make me a bird table for the balcony.

Please come and see me soon.

Love and kisses,

from

Ruby

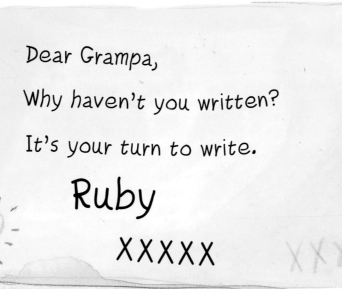

Dear Grampa,

Why haven't you written?

It's your turn to write.

Ruby

XXXXX

Dearest Ruby,

I'm sorry, I wasn't well. I slept for a long time.

Guess what woke me? The magpie family were fighting
by the hollow tree. There were so many I could hardly
count. Seven, I think – 7 for a secret.

They collect all kinds of shiny things
and hide them in their nests.

Here's a shiny secret for you to hide away,
Ruby, my magpie girl:

TOP SECRET

For Ruby only

I'm all right. Don't worry.

Grampa

P.S. I'm making a magpie necklace
for you. When it's finished,
I'll send it.

Dear Grampa,

I'm sorry you weren't well. We've got a secret too – a BIG secret! Guess what? Mum's going to have a baby. I was so happy, I ran on to the balcony and shouted, **"I'M GOING TO BE A SISTER!"**

Dad says he's happy too – except he doesn't know where the money will come from. Babies are expensive he says. Yesterday he took me to the park and we talked about the baby.

I like your secret. But PLEASE look after yourself. (I mean it!)

With love from **Ruby**

(Big Sister!!)

My dear Ruby,

Yes, I heard about the baby and I'm so pleased.
It will be born at Christmas, like a lovely present for
us all. Oh, I wish you could all come and live with me.
There's plenty of room, but you know there's no work here
for your dad. You'll have to wait a little while for
my visit Ruby, because I'm still not quite well.
Anyway, I've had plenty of time to finish your
little magpie necklace. It's made from a branch that fell
from the magpie tree. Now I'm going to paint it –
not just black and white. Magpies have a green and blue
sheen when you look at them carefully. I'll send it soon.
Here's a great big Grampy kiss for you.

X

Dear Grampa,

Thank you for my necklace. I love it. I carry it everywhere.
I take it secretly wherever I go. It's my lucky magpie.
Dad has been home all week. He seems sad.
He says there are too many bills to pay.
I asked him about when he was a boy and he showed me a photo.
He had long black hair, didn't he? He said he used to run through
the woods like a wild animal. Do you remember?

Here is a drawing of the new bird table
Dad made for me. It's just like
a tiny house for all the bird people.
What is your house like?

Lots and lots of love, R.

P.S. Mum says
the baby
can share
my room.

My dearest Ruby,

I'm writing this in bed because I've been poorly.
Yes, your daddy had long black hair and he rushed about as free as a magpie. I taught him to carve wood with a penknife, and now he can make anything.
My hair was black too but it's silver now, just like the song: '5 for silver'.
This is what the house is like. It's an old secret house in the side of the hill. It's got lots of windows that need painting and the roof is wobbly. There are big oak trees all around and that's where those old magpies live. When I see them up there, I think about you on your balcony above the city.
I wish you could fly away to me.
With all my love, from grumpy old Grampa
(stuck in bed).

Grampa,

Now the whole summer has gone and still you haven't been. I hope you're not poorly still? Have you been eating?

Yesterday a horrible letter came. It said they might take our apartment away if we don't pay more money. Mum and Dad were whispering all night – it's *their* secret and they don't want me to know, but I'm scared for the new baby. Will we all live under the railway?

The birds have been coming to the table, but there isn't much food.

Please write soon, because I really want you to.

Love,

Ruby

Dear Grampa,

Why don't you write?
You promised to come.

Ruby

Ruby, my sweet, sweet girl.

There were four magpies this morning
and I knew your brother was born.

The doctor won't let me write any more now
but this is important, Ruby.

DON'T FORGET OUR SECRET!

And don't forget that I love you,

Grampa

Grampa,

Something happened. I woke early because my brother
was crying. I looked out on to the balcony and there was
a big bird there. It looked like a magpie but
magpies don't live in the city. He called to me.

He seemed hungry. Perhaps he'd flown a long way.
Perhaps he'd forgotten to eat.

Then I remembered the song – 1 for sorrow.

Grampa, I'm sad.

You promised to come. Did you send the magpie instead?

Love

Ruby   X

Dear Ruby,

If you're reading this letter,
you've found the secret! I knew
you would. No one else would peep
into the magpie tree.

Show the box to your father.

I carved six magpies on the lid.

You know why.

Be happy,

Grampa

Dear Grampa,

I don't know why I'm writing — just habit I suppose.

We love the house. Dad mended the roof and painted the windows. He put the bird table in the garden. He spends a lot of time doing wood carving now. This morning I heard him singing the Magpie Song.

I am 7 now, but when I run with my brother through the woods, I sometimes feel you are here.

I'll never forget you,

Ruby

Dear Grampa,

There were two magpies on the tree.

Thank you.

Ruby XXX

MORE TITLES FROM FRANCES LINCOLN CHILDREN'S BOOKS

CAN YOU GUESS?
A lift-the-flap birthday book
Laurence and Catherine Anholt

Come to the party and join in the fun! Each spread features
a different riddle. Solve the puzzle, lift the flap – did you guess right?
A lively book of rhymes for parents and children
to read and act out together.

ISBN 0-7112-2214-2 (UK)

ISBN 1-84507-175-1 (US)

HAPPY BIRTHDAY CHIMP AND ZEE
Laurence and Catherine Anholt

Chimp and Zee are monkeying about once more, and this time
it is the twins' birthday party, but will they get there in time?
Presents, games, fun and frolics are guaranteed in this
wonderfully-written addition to the Chimp and Zee series.

ISBN 1-84507-134-4

NOAH'S BED
Lis and Jim Coplestone

It's a stormy night outside the Ark. Little Eber is too frightened
to go to sleep so he climbs into Grandpa Noah and Grandma Nora's
cosy bed. But why is Eber's hair so tickly, and his toenails so scratchy,
and his nose so snuffly? Or is there someone else in the bed as well?

ISBN 1-84507-107-7

Frances Lincoln titles are available from all good bookshops.
You can also buy books and find out more about your favourite titles,
authors and illustrators on our website: www.franceslincoln.com